Dear Parents:

Congratulations! Your child is taking the first steps on an exciting journey. The destination? Independent reading!

STEP INTO READING® will help your child get there. The program offers five steps to reading success. Each step includes fun stories and colorful art or photographs. In addition to original fiction and books with favorite characters, there are Step into Reading Non-Fiction Readers, Phonics Readers and Boxed Sets, Sticker Readers, and Comic Readers—a complete literacy program with something to interest every child.

Learning to Read, Step by Step!

Ready to Read   Preschool–Kindergarten
• big type and easy words • rhyme and rhythm • picture clues
For children who know the alphabet and are eager to begin reading.

Reading with Help   Preschool–Grade 1
• basic vocabulary • short sentences • simple stories
For children who recognize familiar words and sound out new words with help.

Reading on Your Own   Grades 1–3
• engaging characters • easy-to-follow plots • popular topics
For children who are ready to read on their own.

Reading Paragraphs   Grades 2–3
• challenging vocabulary • short paragraphs • exciting stories
For newly independent readers who read simple sentences with confidence.

Ready for Chapters   Grades 2–4
• chapters • longer paragraphs • full-color art
For children who want to take the plunge into chapter books but still like colorful pictures.

STEP INTO READING® is designed to give every child a successful reading experience. The grade levels are only guides; children will progress through the steps at their own speed, developing confidence in their reading.

Remember, a lifetime love of reading starts with a single step!

Go, Dog. Go!

WITHDRAWN

Dogs Clean Up!

by Elle Stephens

based on a teleplay by Brian Clark

illustrated by Dave Aikins

Random House 🏠 New York

Pawston Beach is full
of trash.
Mayor Sniffington asks the
dogs to help clean up.

The dogs who pick up the most trash will get the beach to themselves for a full day.

Tag and Scooch
want to win!

They use a
garbage grabber
to pick up trash.

Frank and Beans
do not want
to clean up.

They play with
the trash instead.
They love messes!
Tag and Scooch try
to stop them.

They clean up Frank and Beans's trash.
Tag and Scooch are sure they will win!

But Spike, Gilber, and Cheddar Biscuit pick up even more trash.

11

Tag uses her

bone-oculars.

They will follow
Frank and Beans
to find lots and
lots of trash!

Frank and Beans
play with piles
of trash.

14

Tag and Scooch
scoop it all up!

They have
so much trash!
They bring it
to the trash truck.

"Wow!"

says Mayor Sniffington.

Tag and Scooch

are sure they won!

They dump their trash bag into the truck.

Frank and Beans
pop up!
They are ready
to make a new mess.

Beans presses a button.
Their trash bin flies
into the ocean.
It starts to sink!

Tag and Scooch
will help.
Tag puts the scooter
in dog-paddle mode.

Scooch launches
the garbage grabber.
"Climb across!"
says Tag.

But Frank and Beans
know it is wrong
to leave all their trash
in the ocean.

They want to help
clean up their mess.
Tag and Scooch pull.
Frank and Beans paddle.

Oh no!

They get stuck.

Tag has an idea.
She sends a rope
to the dogs
on the beach.

The dogs
work together.
They pull and pull.
They paddle and paddle.

The bin is free!
Pawston Beach
is finally clean.

Mayor Sniffington says
Tag and Scooch picked
up the most trash.
They win!

But Tag and Scooch do not want the beach to themselves.

They want all the dogs
to enjoy it.
They throw
a beach bash!

Everyone has a blast—
and picks
up their trash!